CHAIRS ARE TO SIT

by **ESTHER NELSON**

pictures by **JOYCE BEHR**

edited by **DAVIDA HIRSCH**

GRANNY PRESS
New York ✳ New Jersey

Manufactured in the United States of America.
10 9 8 7 6 5 4 3 2 1

The text of this book is set in Century School Book Bold.

The Illustrations are paper cutouts reproduced in the original paper colors.

Library of congress Cataloging-in-Publication Data

Nelson, Esther
Chairs are to Sit / Esther Nelson; illustrated by Joyce Behr.

"A Granny Press book"
184 Central Avenue - Old Tappan, NJ 07675

Summary: A book in rhyme about many things and experiences in a young child's life.
The rhythmic patterns and rhymes are fun, and develop language and auditory skills.
ISBN 0-945110 - 14-6

Look for the companion book "Blocks are to Build".

Website: www.grannypress.com

FOR OUR GRANDCHILDREN

**E.N. * elana * sophie   J.B. * alex * natalie
D.H. * coby * liora * aviva * didi * max**

Chairs are to sit.

Beds are to lie.

Birds are to spread their wings

and fly.

Desks are to write.

Tables are to eat.

Children are to jump up

and down with their feet.

Songs are to sing.

Stories are to tell.

Flowers are to water

and to grow and to smell.

Games are to play.

Dances are to dance.

and prance.

Soap is to wash.

Towels are to dry.

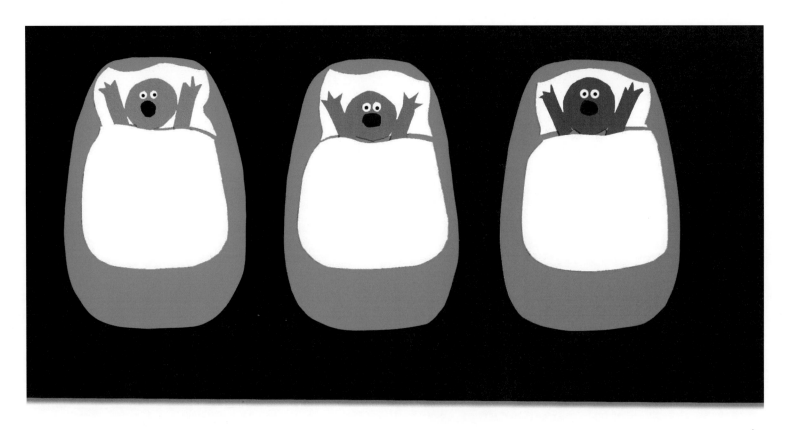

Babies are to

fall asleep bye and bye.

Grannies are to love.

Teddies are to hug.

Kittens are to curl up

snug-as-a-bug-in-a-rug.

Scissors are to cut.

Paste is to glue.

And friends are to play together

ME and YOU!